Terror
At Sea

JUST FOR BOYS™ presents

Don L. Wulffson

TERROR AT SEA

And Other Incredible True Adventures

Illustrated with photographs and prints

Original Title: Incredible True Adventures

DODD, MEAD & COMPANY • New York

This book is a presentation of Just For Boys™,
Weekly Reader Books. Weekly Reader Books offers book
clubs for children from preschool through high school.
For further information write to: Weekly Reader Books,
4343 Equity Drive, Columbus, Ohio 43228

Just For Boys™ is a trademark of Weekly Reader Books.

Edited for Weekly Reader Books and published by
arrangement with Dodd, Mead & Company.

Cover art © 1987 by Weekly Reader Books.
Cover illustration by Dick Smolinski.

PICTURE CREDITS

Department of Agriculture, Forest Service, 88; Department of Defense,
37, 41, 43, 67, 74; Harper & Row, Publishers, 50; Hart Nautical Museum,
MIT, 23; Library of Congress, 47; *London Express* News and Feature
Services, 84; Los Angeles County Museum of Natural History (Jack S.
Grove), 60; The National Archives, 102; National Oceanic and Atmos-
pheric Administration, 57; New York Public Library, 91; U.S. Navy, 98,
106 (Paul Pappas); Jimmie Willis Studio, Waco, Texas, 15, 16, 19, 20.

Library of Congress Cataloging-in-Publication Data

Wulffson, Don L.
  Incredible true adventures.

  Includes index.
  Summary: Includes the experiences of a man caught in a tornado, a
man who sailed around the Arctic in an upside-down ship, a man who
took his family through the "Iron Curtain" in a tank, and a journey
down Brazil's mysterious River of Doubt.
  1. Adventure and adventurers—Juvenile literature. [1. Adventure and
adventurers] I. Title.
G525.W95 1986   904   85-25434
ISBN 0-396-08799-X

CONTENTS

Terror
At Sea

Introduction

Some adventures are ones we plan. How about rowing a small boat all the way across the Atlantic Ocean? Would you plan an adventure like that? Surely, most of us would never even consider such a thing.

Other adventures happen by accident. A few years ago a man was caught inside a tornado. The experience terrified him. True, it was quite an adventure. But no one, of course, would have an adventure such as that on purpose.

These are just two of the amazing stories you are about to read. All are exciting. Some may seem almost too strange to be believed. But nothing is made up. All of these incredible adventures really happened. They are true stories.

1

TERROR AT SEA

During World War II, James Fawley was a prisoner of the Japanese. For eighteen months he worked as a slave in building a bridge in Thailand. He and the other prisoners lived in filth. They had little food. Many died. Though he was sick much of the time, Fawley lived. Back home he had a very pretty wife named Margaret. Dreaming of returning to her was one thing that helped keep him alive.

When the bridge was finished, Fawley and the other survivors thought the worst was over. They were wrong. An even more terrible experience was yet to come.

The Japanese decided to send the strongest prisoners to Japan. There they would work in mines and factories. Though weak and thin, James Fawley was picked out as one of the "strong" prisoners.

He was put aboard a train, in a tiny steel boxcar. Over thirty men were in the car. It was like an oven. Sweat dripped from the prisoners. They licked cracked lips. They begged for food and water. Their guards gave them only enough to stay alive. Finally, after many weeks, they arrived in Saigon harbor. There Fawley and his comrades were put aboard a Japanese cargo ship, the *Rakuyo Maru*. They were beaten and forced down into the hot, airless hold of the ship. The hold was only four feet high. There was not even enough room to stand. All the prisoners could do was to sit or lie down. They were pressed together like sardines in a can. Many prayed for death. They wanted only to be released from their terrible suffering.

Soon the ship was underway to Japan. It

The Rakuyo Maru

was part of a convoy. A great many other Japanese ships sailed with the *Rakuyo Maru.* Day after day they steamed toward Japan.

One night the prisoners heard a strange thud. Then there was another. Ships were exploding. The convoy was being attacked by American submarines. Then two torpedoes struck the *Rakuyo Maru.* The ship shuddered. The bow began to go down. Tons of water poured over the deck as Fawley and other prisoners fought their way out of the hold. The guards were too scared to worry about the prisoners. They let them do as they pleased. It was every man for himself!

When Fawley finally made his way out of the hold he saw many Japanese lowering lifeboats. He also saw men—both Japanese and prisoners—diving over the sides. The ship was tilted crazily. A wave splashed over Fawley. He lost his balance. He slid down the watery deck. He grabbed hold of a railing. He stared down at a sea filled with men and wreckage. It was only a few feet below. He stepped over the railing, holding it from behind. He took a deep breath and dove over the side into the darkness.

Fawley hit the water. The cold shocked him, and he felt a stab of pain in his left leg. He rolled over in the black water. He reached down and pulled a huge splinter of wood from his thigh. For a moment he blacked out. Then, gasping for breath, he dog-paddled toward a dark shape. He grabbed hold of a long piece of wooden staircase blasted from the ship. He pulled—and walked—upward on the thing. Then he lay exhausted. His face was pressed against the wood. He bobbed up and down. Dreamily he watched as more life-boats were lowered from the *Rakuyo Maru*. Then he saw men drifting about him. Some grabbed onto the piece of staircase. Others grabbed onto other bits of junk. Some shouted that they were free at last. Others cried that they were doomed. All rocked back and forth together in the endless, restless sea.

Fawley drifted all night. He thought it would never end. Then, finally, dawn broke. All about him Fawley could see scattered wreckage and lifeboats. And there were hundreds of men. Some were alive. Others floated face-down in the water. He saw one body suddenly pulled under the surface. Perhaps it had been gobbled up by a shark? Fawley didn't know.

A lifeboat drifted by. It was filled with Japanese. "Help us! Help me!" cried Fawley. The Japanese just looked at the half-drowned prisoners. They were not about to help them. The lifeboat continued on.

Several hours later a raft bumped against the staircase. The raft was made of large crates and boxes tied together. Fawley and the others were pulled aboard. As Fawley lay gasping for breath, he watched as a Japanese soldier swam toward the raft. The soldier put a hand on one of the crates. He begged to be saved. But now it was the prisoners' turn to be cruel. Two men kicked and pushed the Japanese soldier away. They did not care if he drowned. He was the enemy. To their way of thinking, he deserved to die.

The sun beat down on the men in the raft. Their faces began to burn terribly. They passed through a huge oil slick from the sunken *Rakuyo Maru*. Slippery goo began to cover the raft and the men. It stung their eyes. It made it hard to hold on. But the worst thing for the men was that they had no water. All began to suffer terribly from thirst.

The day wore on. More men climbed on board the raft. It became packed with survivors and was riding low in the water. And still more came. They pleaded to come on board, but there was no room left. All these poor souls could do was to hang onto the

Covered with oil, dying of thirst, survivors drift on a piece of wreckage in the Pacific.

sides, coated with oil and shivering in the icy water. Some held on for hours, then drifted silently away. With a heavy heart, Fawley watched as they disappeared beneath the waves.

How long can I go on? Fawley asked himself. *How much more of this can I take?* Then he would think of his wife, Margaret, and of home. He was determined that somehow he would make it. Somehow he would return to her.

One day passed into the next. Fawley and the others were tortured by thirst. Some men began drinking seawater. This only made them thirstier. Then it drove them insane. They began to talk crazily and see things that weren't there. One man suddenly pulled himself to the edge of the raft. He pointed out across the ocean. "Look," he said. "There's a restaurant. I think I'll go get myself a nice cup of coffee." He dove into the blue-green waves and swam away. He was never seen again.

The same sort of thing happened a great many times. One man had the idea that the raft was an island and he was sitting by a pool of sparkling fresh water, drinking from it. Again and again he brought handfuls of saltwater to his mouth and drank. A short time later he was dead. Another man said he could see a soft drink machine standing in the middle of the ocean. He swam off toward it and drowned.

For Fawley and the others it was so hard to have water all around, but none of it fit to drink. Once Fawley found himself taking a sip. He spat it out. *No!* he told himself. *No, I'm not going to die like the others. If I drink seawater I'll die.*

Fawley tried to think of possible ways he could save himself and the others. He decided to try to catch a fish. He found a long piece of wire. To the end of this he tied a bent nail and a scrap of shiny metal. To everyone's surprise, a short time later there was a tug on the line. A good-sized fish was pulled aboard. One man had a pocket knife. He cut the fish into small pieces. But when Fawley and the others tried to eat the raw fish they found it was too salty. They threw it over the side.

Fawley put his head down on the oily boards of the raft. He was beginning to give up all hope. It was now his fourth day adrift on the sea and no hope was in sight. He was weak and cold and dying of thirst. His hands ached. From the long hours of clinging to the raft, they were like hard, knotted claws. His eyes stung and were swollen almost shut from the oil. His face and lips were raw and cracked.

Worst of all, he could feel his mind beginning to go. Like the others, he had started to hallucinate. He had started to see things that weren't there. He saw his mother and father. He saw ships and islands. And he saw Margaret, his wife. She talked to him. "Hold on, my darling," she said. "I need you. I love you." He reached out for her. She disappeared.

He closed his eyes. He drifted in and out of sleep. "There's a boat coming!" someone cried. Fawley turned his head weakly and looked about. He saw no boat. "It's a submarine," said the same voice. Fawley closed his eyes again. He had had enough of the madness. He dozed. Then he awoke to find strong arms lifting him from the raft.

"You are aboard the USS *Sealion*," said a man. Fawley looked around. He and the others were on the deck of a submarine! It was no dream. He had been saved. He looked at the man and thanked him. He looked out at the rolling ocean. He saw the raft to which he had clung so long drifting away.

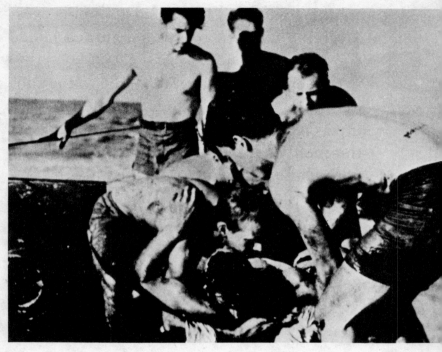

Crew members take a survivor aboard.

He was helped down a hatchway. He was scrubbed with hot water and soap. Then he was helped into a bunk. His mind floated in and out of sleep. The clean sheets and soft pillow filled him with pleasure. He was given sips of water. He ate food. A doctor bandaged his leg where it had been stabbed by the

21

splinter. The oil was cleaned out of his eyes. Medicine was put on his sunburned hands and face.

Fawley got stronger. He talked to the submariners. Pieces were put together. Slowly it was realized that the sub which had saved the men was the same one which had torpedoed the *Rakuyo Maru!* Of course, no one blamed the submariners. They had only been doing their job. And they had no way of knowing that Allied prisoners were on the ship. Fate had just played a very strange trick on one and all.

2

THE MAN IN THE
UPSIDE-DOWN SHIP

In 1757 a ship named the *Anne Forbes* left
the port of Aberdeen, Scotland. It was headed
for the Greenland whaling grounds. On board
was a young man by the name of Bruce Gordon. Gordon had no way of knowing it, but
he was leaving on whát would turn out to
be one of the strangest sea adventures of all
time.

In the Greenland seas, many whales were
taken. The blubber was stripped from them.
Then it was stuffed into barrels and stored
in the hold. Soon the ship was riding low in
the water from the added weight. But the

A whale being harpooned.

captain, a man by the name of Hughes, was greedy. He wanted more whales. Winter was approaching and drifting ice could be seen. Still, Hughes ordered that the ship stay on a northerly course. The sailors, including young Bruce Gordon, began to fear for their lives.

Few whales were seen. None were taken. More important, great icebergs were now all around. The sailors begged Hughes to head back. He only laughed at them. He bragged that he had reached the North Pole. He said the ship could sail as easily to China as to Scotland. Everyone knew, of course, that these claims were utter nonsense.

Then one afternoon the sailors noticed the ship had entered a strong current. It was drifting rapidly northward. Too, a great white fog began to cover the ocean. Captain Hughes suddenly became frightened. He ordered the course to be set to due south.

The current was strong against them. Ice forced itself against the *Anne Forbes* on all sides. The vessel soon became surrounded by the endless floes. For a time they were loose enough to allow slow sailing. Then, suddenly, a vicelike range of ice mountains loomed in the waters ahead. All on board could see that the *Forbes* was heading into the frozen grip of death itself.

Bruce Gordon stood on deck. He watched his approaching doom. Then a hand smacked against his head. It was the hand of his captain. "Up to the masthead," bellowed Hughes. "And keep a sharp lookout!"

Gordon climbed up the frozen wood to the masthead. Everywhere he looked the ship was surrounded by thick white fog and towering bergs. He started to pray. Suddenly there was a tremendous jolt. The *Anne Forbes* had hit one of the bergs. Gordon hung on for dear life. He watched in horror as the ship began to sink by the bow. Huge waves washed over the decks. They swept the men—and all else—into the sea. The whaler listed to port for a moment. Then, in a great sweeping arc, it heeled over to starboard. Gordon lost his grip. He felt himself flying through the air. Something white and cold rushed up at him. He smashed painfully into it. His mind went blank.

When Gordon came to, he found himself lying on an iceberg. He wondered if it was the same one which had crushed the *Forbes*. The *Forbes* itself was nowhere to be seen. Only the floating bodies of Gordon's drowned companions marked the spot where the ship had gone down.

For a long while Gordon sat in a daze. Then suddenly giant bubbles began rising from the sea. The black bottom of a ship broke the surface. It was the *Anne Forbes*! Somehow she had risen again. Upside-down, she very slowly floated away. Then she lodged in a V-shaped cleft of a berg, held firm by a growing clutter of ice.

Gordon knew he was slowly freezing to death. He decided that his only hope of saving himself lay in reaching the ship. He stumbled over ice floes. He fell into the freezing sea. Gasping, he pulled himself forward and struggled toward the ship. Finally, he reached her. He spotted a porthole. He kicked it in. On his belly he pushed forward. He slid down into a cabin. It was the captain's cabin. The place was ice-sheeted and upside-down. The ceiling had become the floor, the floor the ceiling.

Shivering, Gordon looked about. His eyes fixed on an overturned sea chest. He opened

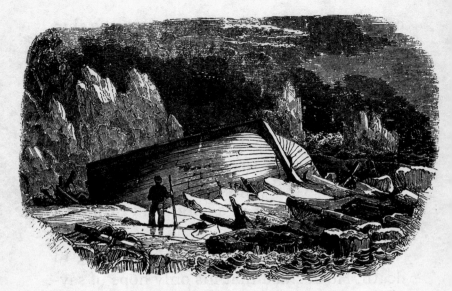

Bruce Gordon studies his upside-down ship.

it to find it filled with a stack of almost-dry clothes. He took off his own clothing. Then he put on some of the captain's clothes. Next, he made his way into the ship's galley, its kitchen. There he found every sort of food. All of it was frozen. He thawed some bread with brandy. Then he ate until his stomach could take no more. He returned to the cabin. He bundled himself in odds-and-ends of clothing. Soon he was fast asleep.

Gordon awoke to some strange sounds. He went to the smashed window. There he saw a dozen or more polar bears. Gordon was afraid. He screamed at them to go away. A few bears turned their heads. One stood up on its hind legs and began walking toward the ship. Gordon feared for his life. He began searching the ship for weapons. He armed himself with a sword and a harpoon. In the galley he found a large fire grate. He hauled it to the entry to the cabin. Then he nailed it in place. To the grate he tied knives, forks, and other sharp instruments, facing them with the points outward. This, he hoped, would keep the bears at bay.

Not for several days were these defenses needed. Then one afternoon Gordon prowled the ship for supplies. Suddenly a giant bear came running at him. A great battle followed. Finally, Gordon killed the animal with a harpoon. Later he skinned it. He used the fur as a rug in his upside-down cabin.

A few hours later another bear found its way into Gordon's quarters. But this was just a baby. It was the cub of the female he had killed and turned into a rug. It went to what it thought was its mother. It lay upon it as though it were still alive. For a long while Gordon just watched the sad little creature. Then he brought it food. He touched his hand to its head. It seemed to forget the rug. It rubbed its muzzle against Gordon. It looked up to him as though he were its mother. Soon it was following him about wherever he went. One day he put his arms around the bear. He hugged it. He named it Nancy.

Long months followed. Gordon continued to live in his upside-down cabin. For comfort he read the Bible and played with Nancy. She was now full grown. But she continued to be as loving toward him as when she was a cub. During this time Gordon also made his quarters as comfortable as possible. He fitted the cabin with a bunk, a desk, and a stove. He felt safe and content. Still, he longed for human company.

One morning he awoke to find the ship

rocking slightly. He looked out his porthole. He discovered the berg to which his ship was frozen had broken free in a thaw. The ship was drifting across open ocean!

For months Gordon and Nancy drifted. Then winter set in. The ship once more became embedded in—became part of—the frozen landscape. They were no longer moving. Nancy lived on the whale blubber in the hold. Gordon lived on the food in the galley.

Year after year, the same thing happened. The ship, still part of the berg, broke free during the warmer months. Then the seas froze over. It was again locked in ice. Gordon began talking to himself. He talked to Nancy. If it were not for her, he felt sure, he would lose his mind. Deep inside, he gave up all hope of ever returning home.

Then one day he found the ship drifting past a giant iceberg. But it was not a berg. It was land! From a mountaintop, men were staring at him as he passed. Gordon waved. The men waved back. Gordon desperately wanted to reach them. But this was not possible. His upside-down ship—and the berg to which it was attached—was still separated by a freezing cold sea. Gordon's heart sank as he and Nancy floated slowly onward.

Months passed. Gordon awoke one morning with a sudden jolt. He scrambled out his porthole. He found the berg had come to rest against a frozen finger of land. Quickly he packed food and weapons. Soon he and Nancy were headed across an icy wilderness in search of a way home.

After traveling many days, he was startled to hear the sound of human voices coming from somewhere ahead. He made his way over a ridge. Then he found himself entering a strange settlement. The people were terrified of him and Nancy. They backed away. Gordon put his arm around the bear to show that she was no danger. Slowly, the people approached.

The people used sign language to communicate. They told Gordon he was in Greenland. They told him they were all that was left of a colony of Norwegians who had

Gordon, after many years, makes contact with Norwegian colonists in Greenland.

settled in the place many centuries before. Gordon then described his own amazing adventure. The people welcomed him—and Nancy—into their settlement. There they stayed for a very long while.

One morning Gordon awoke to find Nancy was gone. The bear had acted strangely ever since entering the settlement. Gordon had not been worried then. Now he was. He searched for her. Days passed. He searched more. He could not find Nancy. She did not return. It was clear she had returned to the wild. It was clear she was never coming back. Gordon's heart was broken. Nancy had meant so much to him. For many years, she had been his only friend.

Gordon was deeply hurt. At the same time, he was more determined than ever to reach home. He bid farewell to the Norwegians. Then he made his way down to the coast. Behind him he dragged a canoe filled with his few belongings. On an empty shore he set up a camp. There he waited for a ship to come.

After several weeks he spotted a whaler. His heart raced. He launched his canoe and paddled furiously toward the vessel. The ordeal exhausted him. He stopped dead in the water. He sat there staring into the frozen, fog-bound sea. He cried out to the ship he could no longer see. Then he hung his head in silence. He felt alone, again abandoned. But an instant later the ship loomed straight toward him!

Minutes later Gordon found himself boarding the *Briel*. It was a Dutch ship homeward bound to Holland. Some of the sailors spoke English. Gordon talked to them nonstop. One of the things he learned from them was that he had been gone almost seven years!

A few weeks later Gordon was in Scotland. He was only thirty-two, but he looked as old as a man of sixty. To anyone who would listen, he told his story. He told his tale of a seemingly impossible voyage aboard an upside-down ship. At first, people laughed at him. They just thought he was crazy. Years went by. Other sailing vessels came back from the Arctic. They confirmed geographical details Gordon had mentioned. In time, his story was accepted by his countrymen. They realized that Gordon had made nothing up. They realized he had survived one of the strangest sea adventures of all time.

3

THROUGH THE IRON CURTAIN IN A TANK

After World War II, most of eastern Europe came under Communist control. The Communists decided they would not allow people to move freely from the East to the West. In some places they put up concrete walls, roadblocks, and fences. Guards patrolled the borders. These barriers—and the Communist policy in general—were dubbed "the Iron Curtain" by Americans and West Europeans. Thousands of people tried to break through it. Some made it. Many did not.

This is the story of just one of these escape attempts. It is the incredible story of Vaclav

Uhlik, who spent three years building a tank in which he hoped to crash through "the Iron Curtain."

During World War II, Uhlik worked in the underground against the Nazis. He sabotaged factories and blew up bridges. One night he was caught. He was sent to a concentration camp. Thousands died there. Uhlik thought he might too. Down to skin and bones, he made a daring attempt to escape. It succeeded. Alone, he managed to get through German lines. He made his way to France. He joined the French army and fought in a tank corps in northern Europe. Until the end of the war, he fought bravely. He fought until the Nazis were defeated.

Uhlik returned to his native Czechoslovakia in 1945. The war was over. The air was full of joy and hope. He thought he was through with wars and invaders forever. He met and married a girl named Marta. He started his own auto repair shop. Business was good. Life was wonderful.

Suddenly everything changed. In 1948, the

Eastern Europeans are held back by a chain-link fence from the West, only inches away.

Communists took over his country. They were against any sort of private business. They closed his shop and took away his license. Though angry, Uhlik was not yet beaten. He still had one truck. He found that he could make some money by cutting trees and hauling them from the forest.

He was getting by. Still, a fury and a desire to be free burned inside him. He decided that he would somehow escape through "the Iron Curtain" with his family. His first thought was to crash through the border barricades in his truck. But he knew that a truck would be shot to pieces by the border guards. Too, the best place to get through was a stretch of swamp. A truck with ordinary tires would bog down in it before going ten yards. What he needed was a tank.

He told his wife Marta and a few very close friends about the idea.

"Oh, Vaclav," said Marta, "where in the world are you going to get a tank?" She laughed. "You are such a dreamer. Such a dreamer!"

Everyone thought he was crazy, but Uhlik was determined to somehow get a tank.

After much searching, he finally found what he was looking for. In a junkyard he came upon the frame of an old British tank. It was stripped of everything. It had no tires, treads, or motor. Only the wheels and steering gear remained. Still, Uhlik was excited. He called over the owner of the place. He said he wanted to buy the rusting hulk.

"What do you want that old piece of junk for?" the man sneered.

"I plan to fix it up. I'm pretty good at mechanics," said Uhlik. "I can turn it into sort of a tractor for hauling wood."

The owner shrugged his acceptance.

Month after month Uhlik worked on the tank. Some of the missing parts he made in his shop. Others had to be purchased. The motor and treads were the most difficult to come by. Then he needed iron plating for the sides. Two friends brought in every scrap of metal they could find. Together the men worked to forge these odds-and-ends into an armor hull. As each item was completed, it was hidden somewhere in the shop. Some items were stashed under piles of rags. Others were concealed behind a cabinet. Some were stowed, dangling by ropes, in the rafters.

Late every night Uhlik and the others

practiced putting the tank together. The first time took over three hours. After six months they could do it in just thirty minutes.

Finally, all was ready for the run at "the Iron Curtain." Besides Uhlik, seven others would be going. In the tank would be Marta, their two children, and four friends.

Almost everything had to be left behind. Even so, it was a tight squeeze for those in the armored hull. Uhlik, in the driver's seat, was the only one who could see out.

Late one night Uhlik, his heart throbbing in his chest, pulled out of the shop into a moonless night. The homemade tank rattled and roared and made a terrible noise. Uhlik gritted his teeth. Those in the hull hugged one another in fear. No one said a word. The tension was too great and nothing seemed worth saying. In less than an hour all might be dead, shot down by border guards. Or, perhaps worse, they would be stopped. They would be captured. All, except perhaps the children, would spend the rest of their lives in prison.

Border guards at a point along "the Iron Curtain."

In the tank they had two guns. They would shoot their way through if they had to.

Three miles from the border they had to pass a camp where 500 border policemen lived. Uhlik had never passed it at night and did not know if guards would be posted. As the camp came into view, Uhlik pushed the speed up to sixty miles per hour. The tank clashed and banged past the camp gate. No one seemed to notice. No one came out.

On and on the tank rumbled. The sky grew lighter. Dawn was approaching. A few hundred yards ahead Uhlik could see the border. They were almost there! Then suddenly Uhlik froze. His heart stood still. At a turn in the road stood a border guard! Looking out the turret of the tank, Uhlik tried to act relaxed. He smiled. He held his breath, waiting for the guard to realize that the tank was something out of the ordinary. At any second he expected the man to raise his gun. Instead, he just waved the tank on. Later, Uhlik commented, "The hour was early. The man must have been half asleep."

But they were not out of it yet. Uhlik still had to lower the treads for the last sprint across the swamp. A hundred yards from the electrified fence, Uhlik jammed on the brakes. Then he pulled on a lever to lower the treads.

A tank similar to the type in which Uhlik and the others made their daring escape.

But it wouldn't move! Something had jammed!

"Help me!" he cried to the others.

One of the men crawled forward. Together they pulled on the lever with every ounce of strength in their bodies. It still wouldn't budge.

"What are we going to do?" groaned the

other man. "If we can't get the treads down we'll never get across the swamp."

Uhlik braced his back against the iron wall of the tank. Then, with his feet, he pushed with all his might against the lever. Suddenly it moved. The treads were down!

There was no time for cheering. It was full daylight now. It was only a matter of minutes before they would be spotted by the military police. Uhlik threw the tank into gear. Ahead loomed the electrified fence. He gritted his teeth and stomped the accelerator all the way to the floor. The engine roared as the heavy iron treads dug into the earth. Faster and faster, the tank rumbled toward the barricade. It hit the thing full force. Wood snapped and chain link toppled. Electric wires tore loose. The air was filled with the sparkle and crackle of electricity.

Dragging part of the fence with it, the tank growled on. Suddenly there was an explosion. The tank had hit a small land mine. It skittered sideways but continued on. Another sharp explosion rang against the steel floor. The people in the hull cried in terror. Uhlik shouted for them to keep calm.

The clumsy vehicle lurched forward into the soft ground of the swamp. It wallowed and slowed to a crawl, but it did not stop. It slogged on through the mire. It churned up onto firmer ground. Then its treads lifted it onto a road beyond the border.

"We made it! We made it!" shouted Uhlik. Joyous cheers rose from inside the hull.

Marta crawled up beside her husband. "Oh, Vaclav, you did it! You really did it!"

He kissed her. Grinning broadly, he turned the tank down the road that would take them to a new life.

4

DOWN THE RIVER OF DOUBT

In the jungles of Brazil there is a large and mysterious river. It was once called the River of Doubt. No one knew where the river went. It seemed to end right in the middle of the jungle. But such a thing is impossible. No river ends that way.

Theodore Roosevelt was the twenty-sixth president of the United States. "Teddy" was also quite an explorer and adventurer. In 1914, after he had left office, he decided he would travel down the River of Doubt. He would find where it ended.

On the dangerous journey Roosevelt took

Colonel Theodore Roosevelt, 1898

his 21-year-old son Kermit, eighteen other men, and a number of hunting dogs. First, the men canoed up the Paraguay River. Then, for over five weeks, they traveled on foot across the highlands of Brazil. Finally, they reached the head of the River of Doubt. Supplies were loaded into dugout canoes. The group set off down the river.

The going was very slow and rough. In some places the river was like a swampy lake. The men had to get out and push and pull their canoes. In other places there were roaring rapids. Sometimes the men would go around the rapids, on land. They hacked through jungle, pulling their canoes behind them. Other times they would "shoot the rapids." They would race down through the churning, fast-moving water. It was both exciting and dangerous.

One afternoon disaster struck. On a stretch of rapids a canoe carrying three men went over. One man was tossed free and managed to swim ashore. But another was thrown against a huge rock. He was knocked out and was sucked under and drowned. The third man was Kermit Roosevelt. He grabbed onto the bottom of the upturned canoe. Holding on for dear life, he raced down a second set of rapids. The boat rolled and he was flung off. For several hundred yards he was swept along in the raging torrent. He passed under an overhanging tree. He grabbed a branch. Gasping for breath, he pulled himself from the water.

A few days later the men found that they faced another terror. The river was full of piranhas! Piranhas are deadly flesh-eating fish with razor-sharp teeth. They attack in vicious, thrashing swarms. In seconds they can turn a full-grown man into a skeleton. The explorers were very careful to stay out of the water and away from these fish. But one day they had to pull their canoes through a marsh. Suddenly one of the men screamed in pain. Moments later a dog yelped and ran away. Piranhas had attacked the man and the dog. As fast as they could, the men made their way onto dry land.

Travel on the mysterious river was never easy.

For the next few days things went better. The canoes made good progress down the river. But early one evening as the group set up camp on shore they saw Indians. The Indians were lurking in the jungle, watching the explorers. Roosevelt and the others expected trouble. But the night passed without any further sign of the Indians. By morning everyone had begun to relax. One of the men even decided to go hunting with his dog. The dog trotted happily ahead into the jungle. Suddenly it let out a cry and went down. There were two arrows through its body! Another arrow smacked into a tree. The man fired his rifle into the greenery. He knew the Indians were there, but he could not see them at all.

The explorers were never again bothered by Indians. But they were soon being attacked by an even worse enemy: insects. Mosquitoes, poisonous ants, and wasps stung them at every turn. The men became ill with malaria. Their hands and feet swelled from bites. Their clothing even began to fall off. White ants ate it right off their bodies!

They had now been on the river over fifty days. They had not expected to be gone so long. Their food began to run out. To keep from starving they had to eat nuts, fruits, parrots, and monkeys.

All of this was too much for one of the men. He went crazy. He started screaming that they would never find the end of the river. It had no end. They would all die in the jungle. He grabbed a gun and started firing into the air. Another man tried to calm him. The crazy man shot and killed him. Then he ran into the jungle. He was never seen again.

This terrible event upset everyone greatly. They began to believe the crazy man's words. They began to think the river really did have no end to it. Too, Teddy Roosevelt was very ill. He had malaria. He seemed to be dying. He told the others to go on without him. "I am only a burden," he told them. "Leave me. You'll do better without me."

The others would not do this. They gave Roosevelt medicine and waited until he was strong enough to go on. Then they again headed down the river. It was smooth sailing. They had no problems with Indians, piranhas, or rapids. Even the insects bothered them less. And fourteen days later they found themselves leaving the River of Doubt and entering another river, the Aripuana.

At last the mystery had been solved. The explorers had found the end of the strange river. It simply emptied into another river. They headed down this river. They reached a settlement. From there they took a steamer back to civilization.

Today the River of Doubt is as rough and untouched as it was in 1914. It is different in only two small ways. For one thing, its route is now mapped and people know where it leads. And it has a different name. It is no longer known as the River of Doubt. It is known today as the Roosevelt River.

5

THEY ROWED ACROSS THE ATLANTIC

For some reason, people are always doing strange, adventurous things. An 11-year-old girl named Becky Gordon bicycled across the United States. Then there was Johann Hurlinger. He walked from Vienna to Paris, a distance of 871 miles, *on his hands*. Another adventurous person was David Parchment. Parchment made 233 parachute jumps—in one day!

But how about rowing a boat across the Atlantic? That would be more than a stunt. The Atlantic stretches 3,000 miles. There are towering waves that could flip a boat over in an instant. There are blinding fogs. Sharks are everywhere. To even think of rowing across this ocean would seem like madness. To actually try it would be like throwing one's life away.

Incredibly, in 1966 two men set out to row across this vast ocean. They were John Ridgway and Chay Blyth. In another boat, two more men, David Johnstone and John Hoare, would be racing to get across in better time. They had already departed, and from a passing ship had come the report that they were making good progress.

Ridgway and Blyth called their boat *Rosie*. She was 20 feet long and 8 feet wide. For sleeping, a canopy rigged on a metal framework covered about half the boat. There was little spare room to move. Most of the boat was packed with food, water, and other supplies.

On June 4, 1966, the men set out from Cape Cod toward Ireland. Day after day they slid up and down an endless roller coaster of waves. One man would row with all his might. When he was exhausted, the other would take over. When night fell, if the sea was calm, a drag anchor would be dropped and both men would sleep on the hard bottom of the boat. In rough seas they would have to row through the night, taking turns.

A few days out a storm struck. Huge waves crashed down on the boat and drove it back toward the United States. When the storm finally ended, the men figured their position. In five days they had traveled only 100 miles. They still had 2,900 miles to go! Certainly Johnstone and Hoare must be doing much better than this. The men talked of giving up and returning home. But they didn't want to be failures. They didn't want people laughing at them. They put their backs to the oars and rowed on.

For the next few days the sea was calm and the sky clear and blue. Then suddenly a hurricane struck. The *Rosie* was soaring up and down waves 30 feet high! The men were terrified. They prayed for their lives. Some food and supplies were swept away. The boat

Ridgway and Blyth, in a 20-foot rowboat, faced 3,000 miles of treacherous ocean.

half-filled with water many times. The men bailed her out. The storm passed. *Rosie* continued on.

Through endless days the men rowed. Their minds went blank. Their only pleasure was the evening meal. As the sun set they would stop and light up their stove. Then they would cook a hot meal. Each bite brought them great pleasure.

At first, both men slept at night. But they wanted to move faster. Ridgway and Blyth decided to row through the night. For two hours one would sleep and the other row. Then they would switch.

Their hands began to hurt terribly. Leg, back, and arm muscles throbbed. To ease their pain, the men talked nonstop to one another. They talked about their families, sports, politics—about anything. Their favorite topic was the meal they would have once they reached Ireland. Over and over they would describe what they would order. Each time, the order changed slightly.

One day a great fog rose up from the sea.

Almost at the same time, a huge whale loomed toward the boat. The creature dived. The men waited for it to come up under them, breaking the boat in half. It never did. But slowly, the thump, thump, thump of a ship's engines growled toward them. Ridgway blew on a pitifully small foghorn. The engines churned closer. The ship was almost upon them! Then they watched it pass. A few yards away was a red and gray hull, plowing through the sea.

The next terror was sharks. Sometimes they followed the boat. Sometimes they swam alongside. They seemed to be waiting for the men to make a mistake, to capsize and make a good mid-ocean meal. Some sharks were so bold they scratched their backs on the bottom of the boat. During this time, it became very hot. Both men wanted to take a dip in the sea. But with sharks all around, they preferred the burning sun.

The skies clouded over. Another storm hit. Ridgway and Blyth rowed into it. They tried not to think of how close they were to death.

Sharks were often about.

In the howling wind, they yelled back and forth. They talked of Johnstone and Hoare, the other two men trying to make it across the Atlantic. They wondered how they were faring. They decided the other men must be doing much better. They would cross the Atlantic faster. But it no longer mattered.

Now, the only goal was to live. On and on into the storm they rowed. Each stroke took them closer to Ireland. Reaching there alive was all that mattered.

Finally, the storm passed. Ridgway and Blyth said a prayer of thanks.

As time passed, the men and their boat seemed to become a part of the Atlantic. Birds set down upon the water or hovered overhead, watching the strange little craft. Dolphins and porpoises dashed under and around the boat. Whales splashed alongside. They seemed to have joined Ridgway and Blyth in their contest to cross the sea. They seemed to be urging the men on.

There were days of storm. And there were days of scorching sun. Little by little, everything on board began to rot and go bad. The men's foul-weather clothes became so worn they had to be held together with tape. Their blankets became riddled with holes. Wet clothing tore apart when touched.

The men began to hate the sea. It became their enemy. It was forever soaking them.

The dampness made their skin puffy and itchy. Their hands felt like clumsy steel hooks. It became harder and harder to close them onto the handles of the oars. Every muscle seemed to harden into a painful knot. Even sleeping was unpleasant. Their boat was so cramped they could not stretch out. Often, when they awoke, their knees ached so badly that tears came to their eyes.

Then food became a problem. Ridgway and Blyth were beginning to run out. Some of their stores had been swept overboard. Some had been ruined by being doused in salt water. Also, the voyage was simply taking much longer than expected. Ridgway began cutting his ration of cheese into little bits. Then he would let each piece melt in his mouth. Sometimes he sucked on candy wrappers, just to taste the sweetness.

At this point, the men had roughly 800 miles to go. Another storm struck. But this one was different from all the others. It helped them. It drove them toward Ireland like a speedboat. In a few days' time they covered a great many miles.

On the morning of September 3, the men saw a thin black line of land on the horizon. They were almost there! It was Ireland! They rowed and rowed with all their might. Then another storm hit. It tried to drive them back. Ridgway and Blyth rowed against it. They saw huge waves breaking against the Irish coast. A lifeboat came out after them. The men waved the boat off. They had come too far alone to want help now.

A few hours later the men touched shore. They had been in the boat so long they could hardly walk. On the beach they staggered about as though they were drunk. They had to be helped. Some kindly people drove them to a hospital.

At first both men felt wonderful. They were terribly tired, but they had done it! They had actually rowed across the Atlantic Ocean. Then came some terrible news. They had won. They had beaten Johnstone and Hoare, but both the other men were dead. Their boat had been found, bobbing, empty, on the cruel surface of the Atlantic Ocean.

Ridgway and Blyth fought against their

feelings. Only they could understand what the other two men had tried to do. Only they could understand the terrors they had faced. Over and over they had come so close to death themselves. So easily, they too could have been lost. So easily, they too could have died while trying to row across the Atlantic.

6

SHOT DOWN BEHIND
ENEMY LINES

Below sprawled the jungles of North Vietnam. As he drifted down in his parachute, Captain Roger Locher's only thought was, *This can't be!* Getting shot down was something that happened to others. Like all fliers, he had never believed it could happen to him. But it had. Unreal as it seemed, it had happened to him!

Locher had taken off that morning from the airbase on his 407th mission. In the rear of the two-man F-4 Phantom jet, he was the navigator and weapons-systems operator. With air-to-air missiles, he had already knocked out three MiG-21s.

66

Suddenly he felt a numbing explosion. "We're hit!" yelled the pilot. The ship flipped over in a ball of flame. It tumbled out of control through space as smoke filled the cockpit.

"I'm going to have to eject," Locher shouted. He pulled hard on the ejection lever. He heard a blast as he was shot earthward. Then there was another blast, a great explosion as the plane disintegrated, taking with it the life of the pilot. An instant later Locher's parachute opened. He blacked out.

He regained consciousness just before he hit the trees. A canopy of green reached up at him. He smashed through huge leafy branches. He felt a bone-jarring tug as his chute was snagged by a tree. For a moment he swung back and forth in the air. Then he unharnessed himself and dropped to the ground.

There was no way he could untangle the chute from the tree. He knew that the MiGs had already spotted him and had probably radioed his position. There was no time to

A Phantom jet over North Vietnam prepares to strike a blow against the enemy.

lose. He scrambled up the side of a small mountain, careful not to leave any trail.

In ten minutes he was gasping for breath. He felt dizzy and his legs were getting rubbery. He crawled into thick jungle growth and lay down to get his strength back. Lying there, he began to realize the predicament he was in. He had no food. He was ninety miles from the nearest pickup area where he could use his radio to contact a rescue team. He was in strange terrain. The enemy was everywhere.

With a compass and a map to guide him, Locher carefully set out southwest. Each step had to be checked for boot prints, broken twigs, or other signs that could give him away.

At noon he suddenly froze. He heard excited yelling coming straight at him. It was a search party of Vietnamese soldiers! He crawled into some thick brush. He lay still as the enemy came into view. He could see their faces. He could see their guns and sharp bayonets. Locher held his breath as the soldiers walked by within a few feet of his hiding place.

The next day it happened again. He heard screams, shouts, rifle fire. *They're trying to scare me, flush me out like a game bird,* he thought. *Stay put. They've practically got to step on you to find you.*

Hunger was beginning to take its toll on Locher. All he could find to eat were a few pieces of unripe jungle fruit. Water was no problem. It rained almost every night. But in the mornings he had to dry out, being careful not to let his boots and socks rot.

Mosquitoes and other insects tormented him endlessly. His skin was covered with red welts and stinging bites. Too, leeches crawled up inside his clothing. Time and again he would pull up his pants to find his legs covered with the ugly things. Their slimy black bodies were bloated with his blood. With disgust, he tore them from his flesh and crushed them.

One nightmarish day passed into the next. Locher grew steadily weaker. He stumbled on through the jungle, not always sure of where he was going. Razor-sharp elephant grass slashed him. Dense brush often blocked his way. Sometimes he pushed through miles of jungle in order to make only a few yards of headway. On the twelfth day he found a wide, well-worn path leading south. With newfound spirit he headed down it. It was a real relief from pushing through jungle brush.

The path led down into a narrow valley. It seemed uninhabited. But suddenly Locher saw two children coming right at him. They were herding water buffalo to pasture. He dove into some bushes. For the rest of the day he lay there in hiding, not daring to move. In the evening, the children began herding the buffalo home. One of the beasts passed within a few feet of Locher. It stepped on a sapling, whacking it down on his ankles. He opened his mouth in pain but stifled any sound.

After dark he wormed his way up the side of a mountain which overlooked a village. Hiding there, he spent a miserable night.

When morning finally came, he pulled a damp, crumbling map from his pocket. With difficulty, he studied it. He found that in twelve days he had gone only seven miles! Ahead of him lay the Red River plain. It was nearly twenty miles wide and filled with small villages. He knew he could never cross it without being captured.

Very weak, and not knowing what else to do, Locher remained in his hiding place. One day fused with another. On the twentieth day he knew he was wasting away. He squeezed skinny arms and legs. He rubbed his buttocks and found only skin and bone. Slowly, the jungle was doing what the enemy could not. It was killing him.

He drifted in and out of sleep. One afternoon he suddenly awoke to the flashes of surface-to-air missiles. They were being fired from the village below at U.S. aircraft. Even if it meant giving his position away to the enemy, he had to let his comrades know he was still alive. He pressed the transmitter button on his radio. Both frightened and excited, he spoke into the radio: "Any U.S. aircraft that reads Oyster One Bravo, please come in."

He switched to receive and heard, "Go ahead, Oyster One Bravo."

The voice startled him. For a long moment

Locher did not know what to say. He laughed. "Hey, I'm still down here after twenty-two days!" said Locher. "Relay that I'm okay."

He switched back to receive. The radio remained silent. He repeated his message. Again there was no reply. His heart sank. No one had heard him. For a long while he hung his head. Then suddenly he was startled to hear another voice on the radio. It was saying, "We've got your position, buddy. Rescue forces on the way. Hold on. We're coming in."

Magically, helicopters appeared on the horizon. They came in high, then swooped down toward where Locher stood. He signalled the choppers by flashing a mirror. He was sure he was only moments away from being rescued. But in the next instant MiGs appeared, their cannons blazing at the helicopters. Then, from the village, antiaircraft weapons joined the battle. In disbelief, Locher watched as the helicopters swooped down low to escape the deadly fire. They slipped over a ridge, then were gone.

It's all over, Locher told himself. He thought sadly of the loved ones he would never see. He thought of the pilots who had risked their lives for him. Sick and near death, he sat down. He rolled onto his side in the jungle muck, waiting to die. He drowsed fitfully the rest of the afternoon and through the night.

In his sleep Locher heard the steady beat of helicopter rotors. He opened his eyes. It was morning. Another pair of choppers was headed toward him! He thought he was dreaming. He blinked. The choppers were real. One slid in toward him. The other held back, ready to act in an emergency.

The lead helicopter hovered fifty feet above him. It began lowering a penetrator, a torpedo-shaped device with enough weight to break through the thick jungle growth.

Automatic rifle fire broke out from the village. The second chopper went into action. It swept down and sideways. Rockets hissed, snaked toward the enemy. Explosions of red and orange billowed skyward,

A chopper of the kind that rescued Locher.

swept back over the village. Mini-guns blazed at the hidden foe.

The penetrator smashed through the over-hanging trees. Broken leaves floated down with it like huge green birds. Locher grabbed the contraption. Trying to hold it steady, he pulled down the seat. He struggled to get into the seat. He slipped and fell. He grabbed the seat again, swivelled sideways into it. Then he felt himself floating, being lifted skyward. The jungle faded below. He looked up. He watched himself being reeled into the chopper.

"Brother, do you look awful!" laughed one man as another pulled him on board. Locher did not know what to say. He was too weak—and too happy—to say anything.

The ride home was the most beautiful journey of his life. The whole way he kept smiling. He looked at the crew and wanted somehow to say thank you. *But how do you thank people for saving your life?* he wondered. There was nothing he could do but look at them with a big loving grin and let the tears roll down through his beard.

7

AGAINST ALL ODDS

Jersey is an island off the coast of France. On October 9, 1964, it was hit by a tremendous hurricane. Trees were uprooted. Houses were blown apart. Thousands of telephone lines were down.

The evening after the storm a boat headed into a Jersey harbor. It was a 53-foot motor yacht called the *Mariecelia*. But there was something strange about the craft. Its deck had been ripped off. Masts, deckhouse, guard rails—all were gone. Still, its engines were running. Suddenly it took a turn and crashed into some rocks. People on the island went to investigate. They couldn't believe what they found. No one had been guiding the boat! No one had been at the tiller. In fact, not one person was on board.

Records were checked. The *Mariecelia* had been cruising the waters with five persons on board. Obviously, all had been drowned. The newspaper headlines that night read: "Five Die in Hurricane."

But all were not dead. Even as people read their newspapers, 21-year-old Alison Mitchell was being tossed about by giant seas, fighting a desperate battle for her life.

Seven days earlier the *Mariecelia* had left port on a cruise. On board were Jim and Dolly Fraser, their son Robert, his friend Mike, and Alison. On the morning of October 9, storm warnings were broadcast to all boats. The *Mariecelia* headed for Jersey, less than forty miles away.

Suddenly a powerful wind began to blow. The sea was turned into a heaving cauldron. Great waves broke over the deckhouse. Glass shattered. Alison Mitchell was badly cut about the head. Dolly Fraser was thrown to the floor and broke her arm. Water poured down into the cabin.

Then a mountain of a wave hissed toward the *Mariecelia*. All on board watched in terror. The wave hit like a bomb. It tore off the deckhouse. Alison had been standing on some steps. The wave sucked her into the vessel; an instant later it flushed her out into the sea. She found herself flailing underwater. Robert grabbed her by the hair and pulled her up. She coughed water from her lungs. She saw Robert and three others bobbing in the waves. All were staring in disbelief at the *Mariecelia*. It was steaming away, still headed toward Jersey. It was going too fast. There was no way they could reach it.

The first to die was Dolly. She had been clinging to a piece of decking, but with her arm boken, she could not hold on long against the heaving sea. Exhausted and in pain, she let go. The others, floating on bits of wreckage, cried to her as she drifted out of reach.

A black wave broke over her. Then she was gone.

"I'm being dragged under!" Mike suddenly shouted. He had tied himself to a beam. As the sea rolled, the beam revolved. Each time it did so it took another turn of the rope. Alison tried to untie him but her fingers were numb and useless. The beam took several quick turns. Mike's head went underwater. Frantic, Alison tried to free him. It was no use. She could not turn the beam or raise him. Staring in horror down into icy water, she could see that he was dead.

Jim Fraser was the next to go. When the monster wave had hit the boat, his nose had been broken. Now tortured by waves slapping into his face, he could barely breathe. "I can't hold on any longer," he cried. His hands slipped from the piece of wood to which he had been clinging. An instant later he was swallowed by the sea.

Darkness approached. Robert and Alison were the only two left. As they bobbed up on the waves, they could see Jersey. With each passing minute they were getting closer to the island. The tide was definitely taking them in. "I can make it," shouted Alison. "I'm going to swim for it."

"I'm with you," answered Robert. "Let's go for it."

Alison struck out for the island. Robert was close behind. Suddenly, Alison felt very alone. She treaded water and looked back. Robert was nowhere to be seen! She swam back and looked for him. It was no use. He too was gone.

Night fell. Alone on the cold, dark sea, Alison kept her eyes fixed on Jersey. She could see the lights from villages. She could see the headlights of cars as they rounded bends in the roads. The island looked so close. She swam with all her might to reach it. But she could make no headway. She realized she was caught in a strong current, being carried eastward. She feared she would be swept past the island, far out to sea.

Mostly, Alison floated on her back. She

81

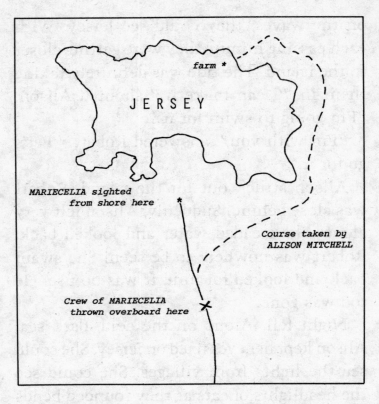

farm *

JERSEY

MARIECELIA sighted
from shore here

Course taken by
ALISON MITCHELL

Crew of MARIECELIA
thrown overboard here

watched as one by one lights disappeared from
windows and from roads. The rest of the world
was going to sleep. Slowly, she was dying.
Up to this point she had never let herself
think that she might not make it. But now
she couldn't go on. She started swallowing
water on purpose. She wanted to die, like all

her friends. Suddenly she spat out the water. She couldn't give up. She must go on. Half-frozen, every muscle aching, she began swimming again.

The long night continued. Alison floated with the current. Her mind and body went numb. Often she was only partly conscious. Still, mechanically, she kept swimming. Gradually, the faint glow of dawn appeared on the horizon. Alison could only half see it. Her eyelids were swollen into tiny slits.

Slowly she became aware of a tremendous pounding and roaring. She was lifted by a wave. She felt herself falling. She crashed into some rocks. They cut and tore her flesh. Another wave swept her free. It tumbled her onto a sandy beach.

For a long while she lay there, letting the surf lap over her. Then slowly, painfully, she crawled from the water. She stood up. Before her was a steep hill. She stumbled forward and found a trail. She began inching her way upward. Often she moved on all fours. She grabbed at roots and rocks and branches. It began to rain. She slipped and slid. She regained her footing, continued on.

Finally, only half-alive, she reached the top. She heard a dog barking. She thought it was the sweetest sound she had ever heard. Then she heard a car. She was frightened and ashamed. All she was wearing was a sweater and panties. The cuts in her head, she could feel, were clotted with blood. Her hair was matted and witchlike. The car rounded the bend. Alison dove into some bushes.

When the car had gone, she heard the dog again. Following the sound, she staggered into a yard. She saw the blurry outline of a house. She beat on the door. It opened.

To farmer William de la Mare, Alison looked like something from another world. From being in the water so long, her body was bloated. Her head and neck were enlarged. Her face was shapeless and her lids were so swollen her eyes seemed to have disappeared. From rocks and flying glass she was covered with bruises, scratches, and streaks of blood.

Alison Mitchell smiles from a hospital bed, recovering from her ordeal.

Alison began to cry. De la Mare covered her with a blanket and helped her into the house. She began jabbering wildly. Words tumbled from her misshapen mouth. It was a long while before she could be understood. Bit by bit, the story she was burning to tell poured forth.

When Alison reached de la Mare's farm it was 11:30 on the morning of October 10. She had been in the water for over 20 hours, fighting for her life while all thought her dead. Happily, the island newspaper had to change its story the next day. Four from the *Mariecelia* had died at sea, not five. Alison Mitchell was very much alive. Against impossible odds, she alone had survived.

8

A RACE WITH DEATH

Deep in the woods of Minnesota is a town named Hinckley. In 1894, as now, most of Hinckley's citizens worked in the sawmill. There they cut trees into lumber. The lumber was then shipped by train to the cities.

On the morning of September 1, 1894, the townspeople awoke to the smell of smoke. Looking off in the distance they could see a huge fire raging in the forest. It was headed straight at the town. People began to panic. They didn't know where to go or what to do.

The sky was turning black. A hot, howling wind began to blow. Fiery cinders flew through the air. These landed on some build-ings on the outskirts of town. The buildings burst into flames.

Many people struck out for a shallow river at the edge of town. Others headed for a big gravel pit. At the bottom of the pit there were always a few inches of water. The peo-ple in both groups hoped to save themselves by dousing themselves and lying down in the water. When the fire passed overhead they would have at least a little protection.

Terrified, the people watched as flames hundreds of feet high roared toward them. Trees lit up like torches in the smoke-filled blackness. A railroad bridge caught fire and collapsed into a ravine. Then the town began to go. House after house burst into flames.

The people realized that they were doomed if they stayed where they were. In a panic, they ran from the woods, then headed down the railroad tracks. This was the only clear pathway through the forest.

At that very moment, a passenger train was headed up through the woods toward

The fire raged through the forest.

Hinckley. At the throttle of the train was engineer Jim Root. Root was on his way to the city of St. Paul. When he first spotted the fire he thought he could race through ahead of it. But as he got farther down the line, he wasn't so sure. The fire was monstrous and fast-moving. Soon the sky became so dark from smoke that Root had to turn on the headlight of his locomotive. He had to lean forward and strain to see the track ahead.

Suddenly he slammed on the brakes. A great mass of people was swarming toward the train. They were fleeing for their lives.

"Please save us!" cried one woman. Her face was soot-blackened and much of her hair had been singed off.

"Hinckley's burning," yelled a man. "And the bridge ahead is gone."

"Everyone on the train," said Jim Root. "Hurry!" He turned to Jack McGowan, his coal-tender. "Tell the other passengers to make room for these people."

As the townspeople of Hinckley scrambled on board, Root tried to figure out what to do. With the bridge down, he couldn't go ahead. The nearest deep water was a place called Skunk Lake. It was six miles back down the line.

Jim Root had only one choice. He gave a long blast on the train whistle, then he threw his engine into reverse. The train began to rumble backwards down the track.

At first, things seemed to be going well. But then the wind changed. Sheets of flame leaped through the forest. It seemed they were racing the train down the mountain. They closed in on both sides of the track. Crossties began to burn. The baggage car caught fire.

Suddenly a wave of fire and superheated air exploded against the locomotive. Every pane of glass shattered. Flying pieces tore into Root's face and shoulders. He wiped the blood from his eyes. He leaned out the window to see where he was going. It was impossible. He was staring into a black, flaming nightmare.

From loss of blood and from breathing smoke, Root grew faint. Suddenly he gasped and slumped over the hot throttle, unconscious. His shirt began to smolder, then burst into flame. Jack McGowan, the fire-tender, grabbed a bucket. He filled it with water from the tank of the locomotive and threw it over the engineer. Root awoke. He looked about

The train raced backwards from the inferno.

groggily. McGowan screamed that they needed more speed. Gritting his teeth, Root shifted the throttle to full open. The train went hurtling backwards, straight through the inferno.

Meanwhile, most of the cars were at least partly in flames. Many passengers panicked, and lost complete control of themselves. One man began running up and down the smoke-filled aisle. His wife tried to calm him. He kissed her. He yelled something, then dove headfirst through a window. A Chinese man and woman crouched in a corner. On their knees, they prayed. Others tried to get them to move to a safer spot, but they wouldn't budge.

Things were no better for Root and McGowan. Flames danced along inside the woodwork of the cab. Big blisters began to sprout on painted metal. Even coal in the tender caught fire. The heat had become so great that Root's face was bright red and his hair smoked and danced with flames. McGowan kept dousing the engineer with water. After taking care of Root, McGowan would move to the rear of the cab where there was more protection. Then he would empty buckets of water over his own head.

Jim Root was near death. His hands were terribly burned. They swelled so much he could hardly move his fingers. Over and over, blasts from exploding fireballs knocked him from his seat. He crawled back so often he lost count.

Still, he held on. He was determined to save the people on his train. Through reddened, swollen eyes he watched the forest pass. Suddenly he slammed on the brakes. Steel wheels ground against steel rails. The train screamed slowly to a halt. Jim Root could barely see, but he knew the landmarks well. He knew he was at Skunk Lake. He watched as the passengers piled off and raced toward the water. Then he passed out.

The lake was surrounded by barbed wire, because it was on private property. People ripped the wire from its posts. The fencing was trampled and kicked aside. Almost 300 persons raced into the water. They threw themselves down into its coolness. They lay there as the inferno roared about them. Many cried. Many prayed. None knew if they would live or die.

Jim Root lay slumped over in the cab. McGowan and two other men pulled his hands from the throttle. They gasped. Root's hands came free, but all the skin was badly burned. They took a closer look at him. His eyebrows were gone. Most of his hair was gone. His face was red and blistered. He was barely breathing. There seemed little hope for him. Still, the men pulled him from the cab and dragged him into the lake. As the fire roared overhead, they held his mouth above water.

Finally, the fire passed. The men dragged Root onto shore. There they, and the other survivors, lay all night.

When dawn broke, Jim Root's train was a smoldering skeleton of twisted metal. But Root himself was still alive. So were most of the people from Hinckley. Jim Root had saved them. Alone, he had driven them backwards from the jaws of death. He was badly burned. He would be scarred for the rest of his life. But he had done something few people would ever forget.

When he had first begun as a railroader, Jim Root's goal was to set a speed record on the rails. He never did this. Both before and after the fire, he tried many times. He always failed. Still, Jim Root did succeed at something even more important. He set a special record all his own. He saved many of the citizens of a town from sure death.

9

FORTY-FIVE SECONDS
INSIDE A TORNADO

It was an overcast morning in May. The year was 1953. Ira Baden gripped the steering wheel tightly as his car sped along a Texas highway. He and Roy Miller were on their way from Dallas to Waco. There they had a job installing automatic doors on the Amicable Life Building.

The men had no way of knowing it, but they were on their way to a disaster. They were headed into a living horror, a tornado. That very afternoon it would strike Waco. In its wake would be left a horrible path of destruction. As many as 114 would be dead.

More than 500 would be injured. Two square miles of the city would be turned into a mass of twisted rubble.

After a long and tiring drive, Baden and Miller arrived in Waco. They made measurements and talked over their plans. Miller began removing the old doors. Down in the basement of the Amicable Building, Baden worked on the new doors. Around four o'clock they were ready to be installed.

Baden and Miller lugged the doors upstairs. They figured how they would set them in place. At the same time, they noticed that people passing in the street seemed quite worried. Everybody was talking about a storm that was coming. The men went to work installing the doors. But it was hard for them to concentrate on the job. The air was strangely heavy and still. It seemed to be pressing down on them. Although it was only afternoon, the sky was as black as night.

"Have you ever seen weather like this?" Miller asked Baden.

"No," he said. He looked up at the dark

sky and shook his head. "I don't like the looks of it. It's really strange."

The men tried to put aside their fears. They kept working on the doors. It seemed like a good idea to get them up as fast as possible. All of a sudden it began to rain. The drops weren't hitting the street. They were flying sideways!

With the rain came an odd roaring noise. The noise became unbearably loud. Then, above the roar, Baden heard the sharp tinkling of breaking glass. He turned in time to see a mailbox flying by. It passed just inches from his head. One pink leg from a store dummy skittered along the asphalt. Half of a store-front sign did somersaults through the air.

The wind was overwhelming. It was like nothing Baden had ever known. He grabbed hold of a railing. For the first time he was really scared. The wind terrified him. He was afraid that he would be torn from the railing and sucked up into the black sky.

As he clung to the railing, a powerful force

began to move up the street. It ripped the fronts off buildings across the way as it came. One place after another simply exploded. Power lines tore loose. They danced in the street, showering sparks everywhere. People leaped and jumped from the deadly lines. Cars braked and swerved away from them. One crashed through a plate-glass window.

Baden tried to get inside the door of the Amicable Life Building. The force of the wind was too great. It had him glued to the railing. He couldn't move. From the corner of his eye he could see Roy Miller plastered against the wall of the building. The man was holding onto the wall with his fingertips.

Baden put his head against his chest. He felt suffocated. The air had been torn from his lungs. Gasping, he blew in and out. It did no good. He could not catch his breath. All the air in the world seemed to have been sucked up into the tornado. Ira Baden was sure he was going to die.

Baden looked up. He could see the ugly, swirling tip of the tornado. It dipped and

The R. T. Dennis Building was just across the street from the Amicable Life Building.

swayed down the street. It demolished one spot and left another untouched. It completely missed the Roosevelt Hotel but reached beyond to level a movie theater. A second later the tip caught the Dennis Building and tore away the top four floors. The

The Dennis Building after the tornado hit.

pieces whirled upward and came apart in the air. Then they crashed down in the same spot. Roofs were popping off buildings. Giant walls collapsed into the street. Cars leaped upward and flew away like airplanes.

In the middle of this shrieking nightmare,

a man suddenly rushed past Baden through the half-finished doorway. Baden shouted for him to stop. The man yelled back that his wife was in the building across the way and he had to get to her. As he stepped off the curb, the wind picked him up. As he screamed, it carried him away. He just disappeared.

Right after that, the wind tore the roof and a wall from the building on the other side of the street. The place looked like a cross-section drawing. Baden could see a man standing beside his desk. He walked to the crumpled edge of the floor and looked over the side. Then he turned and ran to the back wall. He opened a door to what had been a hallway a few seconds before. Then he stepped out into empty space. He was carried up and away by the tornado. Baden never saw him again.

At last the twister began to move away. It was headed southwest, zigzagging off through the city. Baden eased his grip on the railing and looked around. The cars parked on his side of the street were hardly scratched.

Those across the street were something different altogether. They had been thrown around and squashed like bugs. That whole side of the street had been devastated.

The blowing rain continued. It filled the ruined avenue with water. But in spite of the downpour, a crowd of survivors began to gather. Miller put his arm around Baden. Open-mouthed, the two men looked at each other. Then they joined the gathering crowd in the street.

Most of the people were in a daze. Their eyes were blank and their limbs trembled. Some of the people were injured. Others had most of their clothes blown off. One woman put her head on the shoulder of a pale, bloodied policeman. She wept silently.

While he was standing there with the crowd, Baden realized that he still had his glasses on. The tornado had flattened him against a railing. It had picked up cars and blown them away like leaves. It had turned whole buildings into great dusty piles of bricks. Yet his glasses, incredibly, still sat untouched upon his nose.

Rescue efforts went on all night.

The battered remains of Waco the morning after the tornado.

Baden and Miller went to the nearest scene of destruction. They helped to search for survivors. It seemed like a miracle each time they found someone alive beneath the heaps of rubble. The rescue work went on all night. Fire fighters, the National Guard, and others arrived to help.

By morning, Baden was so tired he could hardly stand. Roy Miller was as pale as a ghost. It was clear they could do no more. Behind the Amicable Life Building, Baden

106

found his parked car. He and Roy Miller headed back to Dallas through the battered remains of Waco. In all, Baden had been face-to-face with the tornado for no more than forty-five seconds. But he would never forget those few moments. They would remain etched in his memory for as long as he lived.

DON L. WULFFSON teaches English, creative writing, and remedial reading at San Fernando High School in California. He is the author of *The Invention of Ordinary Things* and *How Sports Came to Be*, as well as numerous other titles for young readers, educational programs, and more than 300 stories, poems, and plays, both adult and juvenile.

Mr. Wulffson is a graduate of UCLA and lives with his wife and two daughters in Northridge, California.